A Bike for Big-Ears

D1337750

HarperCollins *Children's Books*

It was a sunny morning in Toy Town…

Noddy was driving carefully, as usual. But on this particular day he had a very tricky passenger in his car.

"Don't put me off while I'm driving," he told Clockwork Clown, "or we'll have a crash."

"Who, me? I wouldn't dream of it, Noddy," grinned Clockwork Clown.

Noddy stopped at the road junction just outside
Toy Town.

Ting-a-ling-a-ling! Big-Ears rang his bell as he
cycled past.

"Big-Ears must be going into Toy Town to buy
something at Dinah Doll's stall," said Noddy.

Clockwork Clown wasn't listening. With a grin,
he took out a shiny, red balloon and – BANG! –
he popped it! It gave Noddy a real fright.

"Aghh!" he yelled and, by mistake, he put his
foot down on the accelerator. Before he knew
what had happened, the car was skidding crazily
through the streets of Toy Town.

Noddy struggled to stop his car. "Phew!
That wasn't very nice," he gasped.

But just as Noddy turned to ask Clockwork
Clown why he'd played such a silly trick, the
clown leaped up and did a somersault over
the windscreen.

"Thanks for the ride, Noddy!" he grinned.

Noddy was very upset. He'd almost had a crash thanks to that balloon!

"I *do* drive carefully," he said to himself as he drove on, "but it's difficult with clowns like that in the car. I'm a *good* driver..."

CRRUNNNCH!

"Uh-oh! I've hit something!" cried poor Noddy.

"Oh, no!" groaned Big-Ears, who had been talking to Dinah Doll. "My beautiful bike! You've crushed it!"

"I'm so sorry, Big-Ears! I'm really, really sorry!" cried Noddy.

"They don't make bikes like that any more,"
moaned Big-Ears, looking at his smashed bike.

"Don't worry, Big-Ears," said Noddy. "I'll take
it to Mr Sparks. He'll know what to do."

"Noddy's right, Big-Ears," said Dinah Doll.
"If anyone can fix it, Mr Sparks can."

Noddy's face lit up. "And he could add some new things," he said. "A big horn, or flashing lights, or…"

"No horns. No flashing lights," said Big-Ears, firmly.

"But Big-Ears…" cried Noddy.

"No, Noddy. I don't want anything new. My bike was perfect just as it was."

"Oh, all right," said Noddy.

Noddy took Big-Ears' bike to the Toy Town garage.

"Can you fix it, Mr Sparks?" he asked.

"Of course, Noddy, I'll make it as good as new."

"I bet you could make it even better!" said
Noddy. "But Big-Ears wants his old bike back
just as it was."

"Some people don't like change," said Mr Sparks.

"I feel bad about wrecking his bike, Mr Sparks,"
said Noddy. "Is there any way you could make it
better than it was?"

"Hmm," said Mr Sparks. "Ah-ha, I do have an
idea, Noddy. I could fit Big-Ears' bike with a motor."

"Oh, *yes*, Mr Sparks!" Noddy was thrilled.
"A motor would make his bike much more fun."

"Can you hide the motor in this basket?" Noddy asked. "Then Big-Ears'll get a real surprise when he starts pedalling."

"Fitting a motor in a basket is quite a challenge," said Mr Sparks, "...but I like it!" And he rolled up his sleeves and got started.

Happy now, Noddy skipped out of the garage, singing:

> Count on me, any time at all,
> I will always answer when you call.
> Count on me, I will see you through,
> And I know that I can count on you!

Later, Noddy took the mended bike to Big-Ears at Toadstool House.

"Here it is, Big-Ears," said Noddy, proudly.

"Ahh!" Big-Ears gasped. "It's beautiful! Thank you, Noddy. But what's this? I thought I asked you not to add anything new."

"It's only a basket, Big-Ears, and…"

"I love it, Noddy! It's what I've always wanted," said Big-Ears, smiling.

"It's a *special* kind of basket, Big-Ears," Noddy
started to explain. "To make you go faster!"

"You are funny, Noddy," Big-Ears chuckled.
"A basket can't make my bike go any faster!"

"Just try it!" said Noddy, eagerly.

"If Mr Sparks fixed my bike, I'm sure it's as
good as new, Noddy," said Big-Ears.

"It's *better* than new, Big-Ears. Much better!"
cried Noddy.

"You're right, Noddy," said Big-Ears as he began
to pedal his bike. "Mr Sparks did a great job."

He rode slowly around Noddy.

"Faster, Big-Ears. Pedal faster!" cried Noddy.

"All right, I will," said Big-Ears.

"Thundering toadstools! It's ALIVE!" cried
poor Big-Ears as his pedalling kick-started
the motor-in-a-basket.

"Aaghh!" he shrieked as the bike roared away.
"Watch out, Noddy. I can't stop! HELP!"

Big-Ears tried his best to steer, but his bike was going too fast. It swerved around Noddy and zoomed off down the road towards Toy Town, with Big-Ears clinging on for dear life.

Noddy jumped into his little car and tore after Big-Ears.

"Quick, little car, we've got to rescue Big-Ears!"
cried Noddy, chasing after the runaway bike.

As Noddy raced along, he shouted, "Slow
down, Big-Ears!"

"I caaaaaan't!" yelled Big-Ears.

Big-Ears, on the runaway bike, hurtled past Clockwork Clown.

Then Noddy whizzed by.

"Whooahh!" Clockwork Clown was whirled round by the whoosh of air from the car.

"Oops! Sorry!" yelled Noddy. "Can't stop!"

"Any minute now," cried Noddy in a panic, "we'll be in the middle of Toy Town's busy streets!"

Ting-a-ling-a-ling! Big-Ears rang his bell madly, warning everyone to get out of his way.

"Sorry!" he shouted as he shot past Mr Wobbly Man and sent him spinning across the road.

"Look out! Coming through!" Big-Ears yelled as
he bounced off a rubbish bin, ran over a little
tree, then whizzed past Clockwork Mouse,
Mr Jumbo, Dinah Doll and Tessie Bear.

"Looks like Mr Sparks got that bike working
a little *too* well," said Dinah Doll.

At top speed, Big-Ears roared straight into
Mr Sparks' open garage.

CRASH! BANG! BUMP! THUMP! CRUNCH!

Tools, bits and pieces of cars and bikes flew
through the air as Big-Ears smashed into the
workshop – and out again.

"Help!" wailed Big Ears. "I can't hold on much longer!"

Noddy had to do something – and fast!

He drove up behind his old friend, yelling, "When I say, 'Now!' Big-Ears, jump into my car!"

"OK!" Big-Ears gasped. "Just get me off this thing!"

It wasn't easy to drive alongside the runaway
bike, but Noddy managed it.

"Ready... NOW!" he shouted.

Big-Ears leaped off his bike – and into Noddy's car.

He was safe at last, thanks to Noddy's brave and clever driving. His bike zoomed straight into a wall. KERRUNCH!

Big-Ears' bike was smashed again. But at least the motor-in-a-basket had finally stopped.

"I'm sorry, Big-Ears. I wanted to make your bike better. So I asked Mr Sparks to put a motor on it."

"So I see, Noddy," said Big-Ears. "Next time you want to help someone, do what they ask for, not what you think is best for them!"

"I will," said Noddy. "I'll ask Mr Sparks to mend your bike just the way you like it."

Then Noddy grinned. "Are you *sure* you don't want any flashing lights, Big-Ears?" he asked.

"You funny little Noddy," said Big-Ears. "You know I don't."

And they both laughed until the bell on Noddy's hat jingled.

This edition produced for The Book People Ltd,
Hall Wood Avenue, Haydock, St Helens, WA11 9UL
First published in Great Britain by HarperCollins Publishers Ltd in 2002

1

This edition published by HarperCollins Children's Books
HarperCollins Children's Books is a division of HarperCollins Publishers Ltd.

Text and images copyright © 2002 Enid Blyton Ltd (a Chorion company).
The word "NODDY" is a registered trade mark of Enid Blyton Ltd. All rights reserved.
For further information on Noddy please contact www.NODDY.com

ISBN: 978 0 00 783063 3

Visit our website at: www.harpercollinschildrensbooks.co.uk

Printed and bound by South China Printing Co. Ltd